P9-BYL-216

A Note to Parents

Read to your child...

★ Reading aloud is one of the best ways to develop your child's love of reading. Older readers still love to hear stories.

★ Laughter is contagious. Read with feeling. Show your child that reading is fun.

★ Take time to answer questions your child may have about the story. Linger over pages that interest your child.

...and your child will read to you.

★ Do not correct every word your child misreads. Say, "Does that make sense? Let's try it again."

★ Praise your child as he progresses. Your encouraging words will build his confidence.

You can help your Level 2 reader.

★ Keep the reading experience interactive. Read part of a sentence, then ask your child to add the missing word.

★ Read the first part of a story, then ask your child, "What's going to happen next?"

★ Give clues to new words. Say, "This word begins with *b* and ends in *ake*, like *rake, take, lake*."

★ Ask your child to retell the story using her own words.

★ Use the five *W*s: WHO is the story about? WHAT happens? WHERE and WHEN does the story take place? WHY does it turn out the way it does?

Most of all, enjoy your reading time together!

Fisher-Price and related trademarks and copyrights
are used under license from Fisher-Price, Inc.,
a subsidiary of Mattel, Inc., East Aurora, NY 14052. U.S.A.
©2003 Mattel, Inc. All Rights Reserved
Reader's Digest Children's Books
Reader's Digest Road, Pleasantville, NY 10570-7000
Copyright © 2003 Reader's Digest Children's Publishing, Inc.
All rights reserved. Reader's Digest Children's Books is a trademark
and Reader's Digest and All-Star Readers are registered trademarks
of The Reader's Digest Association, Inc.
Printed in China.
10 9 8 7 6 5 4 3 2 1

Library of Congress Cataloging-in-Publication Data

Mitter, Matt
  It's day one hundred!/ by Matt Mitter ; illustrated by Anne Kennedy.
    p.   cm. — (All-star readers. Level 2)
  Summary: Students, teachers, and their principal celebrate Day One Hundred
with a special song, one hundred exercises, festive food, posters, and more.
  ISBN 0-7944-0204-6 (pbk. : alk. paper)
  [1. Schools—Fiction. 2. Counting—Fiction. 3. Hundred (The number)—Fiction. 4.
Stories in rhyme.] I. Kennedy, Anne, ill. II. Title. III. Series.
PZ8.3.M684It 2003   [E]—dc21   2002031903

The 100th Day of School!

by Matt Mitter
illustrated by Anne Kennedy

T 55963

All-Star Readers®

Reader's Digest Children's Books™
Pleasantville, New York • Montréal, Québec

At last, it's here! It's here at last.
We've been counting since day one.
We counted ninety-nine long days.
Now Day One Hundred has begun!

Everyone is dressed for fun
in silly hats and silly clothes.
Look! Molly's mother tied her hair
with one hundred little bows!

Some teachers dressed to look
one hundred—
wearing beards and walking slow!

Miss Lane dressed like ladies did at least one hundred years ago!

Principal Jones makes a speech that's one hundred words long!

And then she leads us as we sing our special "Day One Hundred Song."

The Day One Hundred Song

Day One Hundred's here at last,
the day we've waited for.
We worked and worked one hundred day
We now know so much more.

Day One Hundred's here at last!
Time for us to have some fun!
We've learned so much since we beg
together on day one!

The song is sung.
We cheer and clap.
The "Count One Hundred"
now begins!

We count by ones.
We count by fives.
Then we count again by tens!

Five, ten, fifteen, twenty,
twenty-five, thirty, thirty-five,
forty, forty-five, fifty, fifty-five,
sixty, sixty-five, seventy,
seventy-five, eighty, eighty-five,
ninety, ninety-five,
ONE HUNDRED!

Ten, twenty, thirty, forty, fifty, sixty, seventy, eighty, ninety, ONE HUNDRED!

Now "Day One Hundred Exercises"
led outside by Coach McCall.
Ten exercises—ten times each.

That makes one hundred—
whew!—in all!

We cover every classroom wall
with one hundred posters, too!

We must use up one hundred miles of tape before we're through!

Each day we learn
one spelling word—
so what will Day One Hundred's be?

Slowly teacher writes it down
That's it! It's C-O-U-N-T!

Word of the day—

count

Day 100!

It's time for
"Eat One Hundred Lunch."
Our plates are filled
with funny things!

It all looks like one hundred. See?
A hot dog next to onion rings!

We each have brought
one hundred things.
There are pennies, sticks,
and stones.

Joe even brought his
dog's collection
of one hundred chewy bones!

At three o'clock we go outside
as Day One Hundred closes.
And all around our school we plant
one hundred bright red roses.

And once the last red rose
is planted,
Day One Hundred's finally done.

Tomorrow can we do it all
again for Day One Hundred One?

Words are fun!

Here are some simple activities you can do with a pencil, crayons, and a sheet of paper. You'll find the answers at the bottom of the page.

———— ★ ————

1. Match the scrambled words with the correctly spelled words on the right.

lpels	song
sreay	lunch
nogs	spell
cnulh	years

2. What happened next? Put the sentences below in the order things occurred in the story.

a. One hundred red roses are planted at three o'clock.

b. Principal Jones makes a speech.

c. The school sings the "Day One Hundred Song."

d. Day One Hundred begins.

e. The school has "Eat One Hundred Lunch."

3. Circle the two words that rhyme in each line.

nose	card	bows
wig	pig	nail
watch	near	cheer
five	dive	frame
things	lamp	rings

4. Each student brought one hundred things to school. Wha might you bring? Draw a picture of your collection

5. Circle the action word in each line.

eat	day	together
balloon	hat	count
speech	clap	outside
miles	dog	work

ANSWERS:
1. lpels=spell; sreay=years; nogs=song; cnulh=lunch
2. d, b, c, e, a
3. nose=bows; wig=pig; near=cheer; five=dive; things=rings
5. eat; count; clap; work

2-3
Mitter

Fairbury Public Library
601 7th St.
Fairbury, NE 68352

Date Due

JUN 04 2004	OCT 1 0 2014		
JUN 15 2004	FEB 0 3 2015		
JUL 1 2004	JUN 4 2015		
NOV 1 2004	FEB 8 2016		
JUN 2 8 2005			
SEP 1 3 2005			
OCT 2 8 2006			
JAN 2 7 2009			
2-13-09			
FEB 4 2010			
FEB 4 2010			
Feb 21, 2010			
JAN 3 1 2012			
JAN 3 1 2012			
FEB 1 1 2014			

BRODART, CO.   Cat. No. 23-233-003   Printed in U.S.A.